For my girl, Claude,
with all my love.

Visit us on the Web! rhcbooks.com
Educators and librarians, for a variety of teaching tools, visit us at RHTeachersLibrarians.com
Library of Congress Cataloging-in-Publication Data
Names: Masi, Dawn, author, illustrator.
Title: G my name is girl / by Dawn Masi.
Description: First edition. | New York : Doubleday, [2021] | Audience: Ages 3–7. | Summary:
Illustrations and rhythmic text celebrate girls around the world and what makes each an individual,
from adventurous Argentines Alba and Ayelén to zealous Zambians Zahra and Zena.
Identifiers: LCCN 2020009836 (print) | LCCN 2020009837 (ebook)
ISBN 978-0-593-30404-4 (hardcover) | ISBN 978-0-593-30405-1 (library binding) |
ISBN 978-0-593-30406-8 (ebook)
Subjects: CYAC: Girls—Fiction. | Individuality—Fiction. | Alphabet.
Classification: LCC PZ7.1.M3755 Gam 2021 (print) | LCC PZ7.1.M3755 (ebook) | DDC [E]—dc23
MANUFACTURED IN CHINA
10 9 8 7 6 5 4 3 2 1
First Edition

G MY NAME
IS GIRL

Written and illustrated by

DAWN MASI

Doubleday Books
for Young Readers

Throughout the land, across the sea, let's find friends from **A** to **Z**.
Take my hand—one, two, three! Skip and hop and jump with me. . . .

A, my name is **ALBA**,
and my sister's name is **AYELÉN**.
We come from **ARGENTINA**,
and we are **ADVENTUROUS**.

B, my name is **BINTOU**,
and my best friend's name is **BERTILLE**.
We come from **BURKINA FASO**,
and we are **BRAVE**.

C, my name is **CLARA**, and my neighbor's name is **CLAUDIA**.
We come from **CUBA**, and we are **CREATIVE**.

D, my name is **DITTE**,
and my cousin's name is **DANNA**.
We come from **DENMARK**,
and we are **DETERMINED**.

E, my name is **ESHE**, and my mother's name is **EMAN**.
We come from **ETHIOPIA**, and we are **EMPATHETIC**.

F, my name is **FRANCES**, and my grandma's name is **FELISE**.
We come from **FIJI**, and we are **FEARLESS**.

G, my name is **GAEA**, and my best friend's name is **GRETA**.
We come from **GREECE**, and we are **GRACEFUL**.

H, my name is **HANNA**, and my sister's name is **HONORINE**.
We come from **HAITI**, and we are **HEROIC**.

I, my name is **INDU**, and my niece's name is **ISHANI**.
We come from **INDIA**, and we are **INVENTIVE**.

J, my name is **JURI**, and my grandmother's name is **JUN**.
We come from **JAPAN**, and we are **JUBILANT**.

K, my name is **KEYLAH**, and my neighbor's name is **KYALO**.
We come from **KENYA**, and we are **KINDHEARTED**.

L, my name is **LAE**, and my auntie's name is **LULANI**.
We come from **LAOS**, and we are **LOVING**.

M, my name is **MITZI**, and my mama's name is **MAYELA**.
We come from **MEXICO**, and we are **MINDFUL**.

N, my name is **NELLY**, and my granny's name is **NINA**.
We come from **NEW ZEALAND**, and we are **NURTURING**.

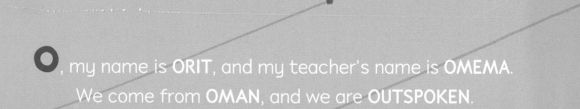

O, my name is **ORIT**, and my teacher's name is **OMEMA**.
We come from **OMAN**, and we are **OUTSPOKEN**.

N, my name is **NELLY**, and my granny's name is **NINA**.
We come from **NEW ZEALAND**, and we are **NURTURING**.

O, my name is **ORIT**, and my teacher's name is **OMEMA**.
We come from **OMAN**, and we are **OUTSPOKEN**.

P, my name is **PAOLA**, and my teammate's name is **PALOMA**. We come from **PERU**, and we are **PASSIONATE**.

Q, my name is **QINDEEL**, and my best friend's name is **QAMIRAH**.
We come from **QATAR**, and we are **QUICK-WITTED**.

R, my name is **ROZA**, and my mother's name is **RENATA**.
We come from **RUSSIA**, and we are **RADIANT**.

S, my name is **SAYA**, and my auntie's name is **SIMA**.
We come from **SYRIA**, and we are **STRONG**.

T, my name is **TICHA**, and my classmate's name is **TANAYA**.
We come from **THAILAND**, and we are **TALENTED**.

U, my name is **UMA**, and my girlfriend's name is **ULLA**.
We come from the **USA**, and we are **UNABASHED**.

V, my name is **VILMA**, and my sister's name is **VALERIA**.
We come from **VENEZUELA**, and we are **VOCAL**.

W, my name is **WENDA**, and my best friend's name is **WYNNE**.
We come from **WALES**, and we are **WISHFUL**.

X, my name is **AXELLE**, and my nana's name is **MAXINE**.
We come from **LUXEMBOURG**, and we are **EXTRAORDINARY**.

Y, my name is **YARA**,
and my cousin's name is **YASMIN**.
We come from **YEMEN**,
and we are **YOUNG** (BUT WISE).

Z, my name is **ZAHRA**, and my sister's name is **ZENA**.
We come from **ZAMBIA**, and we are **ZEALOUS**.

Now it's your turn. Join our crew.
Tell me your name and what makes you **YOU**!

FOR STELLA & SAM—

MAY YOU ALWAYS PARDON EACH OTHER

 SIMON & SCHUSTER BOOKS FOR YOUNG READERS • An imprint of Simon & Schuster Children's Publishing Division • 1230 Avenue of the Americas, New York, New York 10020 • Copyright © 2014 by Daniel Miyares • All rights reserved, including the right of reproduction in whole or in part in any form. • SIMON & SCHUSTER BOOKS FOR YOUNG READERS is a trademark of Simon & Schuster, Inc. • For information about special discounts for bulk purchases, please contact Simon & Schuster Special Sales at 1-866-506-1949 or business@simonandschuster.com. • The Simon & Schuster Speakers Bureau can bring authors to your live event. For more information or to book an event, contact the Simon & Schuster Speakers Bureau at 1-866-248-3049 or visit our website at www.simonspeakers.com. • Book design by Chloë Foglia • The text for this book is hand lettered. • The illustrations for this book are rendered in digital mixed media. Manufactured in China • 0314 SCP

2 4 6 8 10 9 7 5 3 1

Library of Congress Cataloging-in-Publication Data • Miyares, Daniel, author, illustrator. • Pardon me! / Daniel Miyares. — First edition. • pages cm • Summary: A bird tries to keep his spot to himself only to discover that spot is not so safe. • ISBN 978-1-4424-8997-4 (hardcover) — ISBN 978-1-4424-8998-1 (eBook) • [1. Birds—Fiction. 2. Sharing—Fiction.] I. Title. • PZ7.M699577Par 2014 • [E]—dc23 • 2013006081

first edition

PARDON ME!

BY DANIEL MIYARES

SIMON & SCHUSTER BOOKS FOR YOUNG READERS
NEW YORK   LONDON   TORONTO   SYDNEY   NEW DELHI

Pardon me.

WELL, I SUPPOSE I CAN'T STOP YOU.

Pardon me.

IT'S CROWDED ALREADY, DON'T YOU THINK?

Pardon me.

SURE. THE ENTIRE SWAMP'S HERE ALREADY. WHY SHOULDN'T YOU BE TOO?

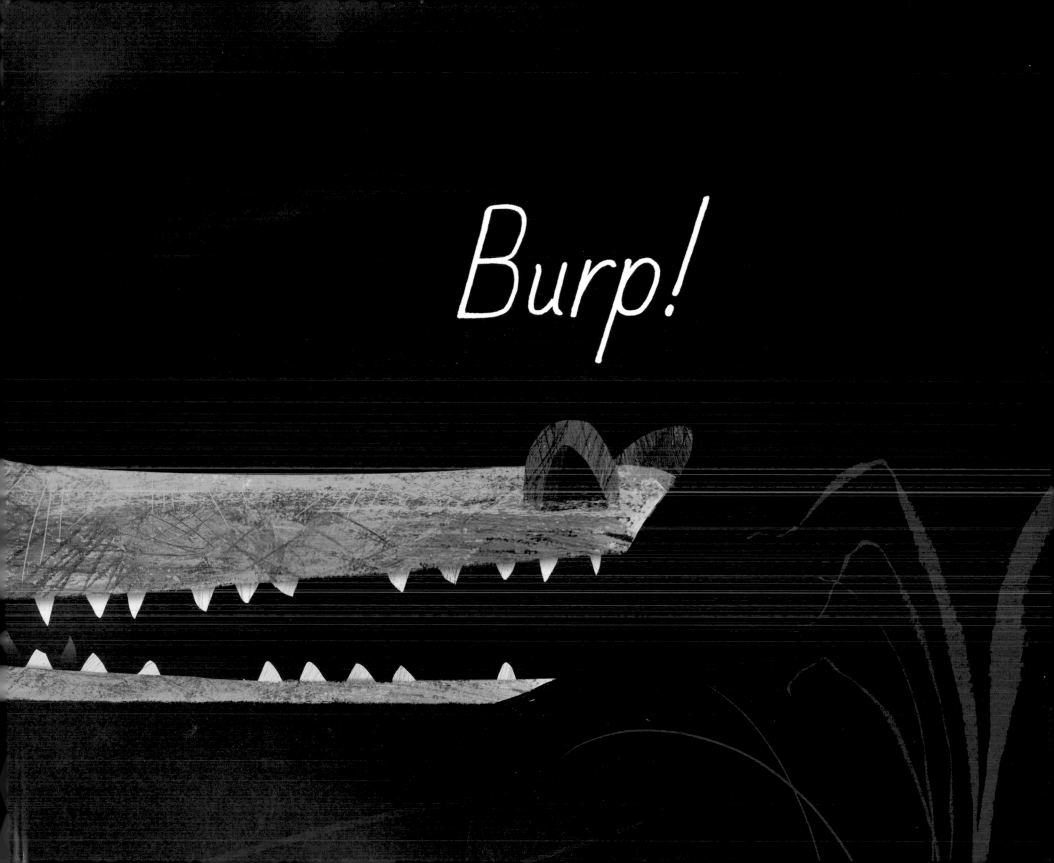

Pardon me.